The world's greatest _fitness_ game

No Pain, No Gain Mad Libs

by Laura Marchesani

PRICE STERN SLOAN
An Imprint of Penguin Group (USA) LLC

PRICE STERN SLOAN
Published by the Penguin Group
Penguin Group (USA) LLC, 375 Hudson Street, New York 10014, USA

USA | Canada | UK | Ireland | Australia | New Zealand | India | South Africa | China

penguin.com
A Penguin Random House Company

Mad Libs format and text copyright © 2014 by Price Stern Sloan, an imprint of Penguin Group (USA) LLC. All rights reserved.

Published by Price Stern Sloan,
a division of Penguin Young Readers Group,
345 Hudson Street, New York 10014.
Printed in the USA.

Penguin supports copyright. Copyright fuels creativity, encourages diverse voices, promotes free speech, and creates a vibrant culture. Thank you for buying an authorized edition of this book and for complying with copyright laws by not reproducing, scanning, or distributing any part of it in any form without permission. You are supporting writers and allowing Penguin to continue to publish books for every reader.

ISBN 978-0-8431-8051-0

1 3 5 7 9 10 8 6 4 2

PSS! and *MAD LIBS* are registered trademarks of Penguin Group (USA) LLC.
ADULT MAD LIBS is a trademark of Penguin Group (USA) LLC.

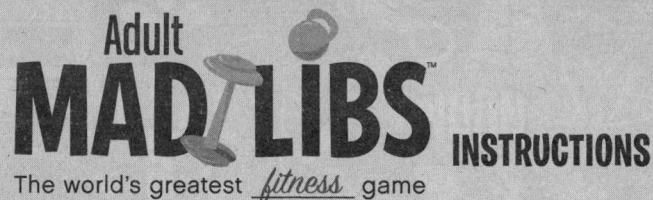

INSTRUCTIONS

The world's greatest _fitness_ game

MAD LIBS® is a game for people who don't like games! It can be played by one, two, three, four, or forty.

• RIDICULOUSLY SIMPLE DIRECTIONS

In this book, you'll find stories containing blank spaces where words are left out. One player, the READER, selects one of the stories. The READER shouldn't tell anyone what the story is about. Instead, the READER should ask the other players, the WRITERS, to give words to fill in the blank spaces in the story.

• TO PLAY

The READER asks each WRITER in turn to call out words—adjectives or nouns or whatever the spaces call for—and uses them to fill in the blank spaces in the story. The result is your very own MAD LIBS! Then, when the READER reads the completed MAD LIBS to the other players, they will discover they have written a story that is fantastic, screamingly funny, shocking, silly, crazy, or just plain dumb—depending on the words each WRITER called out.

• EXAMPLE (*Before* and *After*)

"_____!" he said _____
    EXCLAMATION   ADVERB

as he jumped into his convertible _____ and
                                      NOUN

drove off with his _____ wife.
                      ADJECTIVE

"_____*Ouch*_____!" he said _____*stupidly*_____
    EXCLAMATION   ADVERB

as he jumped into his convertible _____*cat*_____ and
                                      NOUN

drove off with his _____*brave*_____ wife.
                      ADJECTIVE

Adult MAD LIBS

The world's greatest *fitness* game

QUICK REVIEW

In case you have forgotten what adjectives, adverbs, nouns, and verbs are, here is a quick review:

An **ADJECTIVE** describes something or somebody. *Lumpy, soft, ugly, messy*, and *short* are adjectives.

An **ADVERB** tells how something is done. It modifies a verb and usually ends in "ly." *Modestly, stupidly, greedily*, and *carefully* are adverbs.

A **NOUN** is the name of a person, place, or thing. *Sidewalk, umbrella, bridle, bathtub*, and *nose* are nouns.

A **VERB** is an action word. *Run, pitch, jump*, and *swim* are verbs. Put the verbs in past tense if the directions say **PAST TENSE**. *Ran, pitched, jumped*, and *swam* are verbs in the past tense.

When we ask for **A PLACE**, we mean any sort of place: a country or city (*Spain, Cleveland*) or a room (*bathroom, kitchen*).

An **EXCLAMATION** or **SILLY WORD** is any sort of funny sound, gasp, grunt, or outcry, like *Wow!, Ouch!, Whomp!, Ick!*, and *Gadzooks!*

When we ask for specific words, like a **NUMBER**, a **COLOR**, an **ANIMAL**, or a **PART OF THE BODY**, we mean a word that is one of those things, like *seven, blue, horse*, or *head*.

When we ask for a **PLURAL**, it means more than one. For example, *cat* pluralized is *cats*.

Adult MAD LIBS™
LOCKER ROOM ETIQUETTE

The world's greatest *fitness* game

MAD LIBS® is fun to play with friends, but you can also play it by yourself! To begin with, DO NOT look at the story on the page below. Fill in the blanks on this page with the words called for. Then, using the words you have selected, fill in the blank spaces in the story. Now you've created your own hilarious MAD LIBS® game!

A PLACE _____

PLURAL NOUN _____

ADJECTIVE _____

ADJECTIVE _____

PLURAL NOUN _____

ARTICLE OF CLOTHING _____

ADJECTIVE _____

ADVERB _____

PART OF THE BODY (PLURAL) _____

ARTICLE OF CLOTHING _____

PART OF THE BODY _____

ADJECTIVE _____

NOUN _____

NUMBER _____

VERB _____

NOUN _____

LOCKER ROOM ETIQUETTE

The locker room at (the) _____ is usually crowded with tons
                          A PLACE
of sweaty _____. It's important to practice _____
          PLURAL NOUN   ADJECTIVE
etiquette in order to make your experience at the gym as
_____ as possible. For one thing, if there's only one or two
 ADJECTIVE
_____ to sit on, don't leave your stuff all over them. No
 PLURAL NOUN
one wants to sit next to your sweaty _____ while they're
                                      ARTICLE OF CLOTHING
trying to put their sneakers on. Obviously you're going to have to
get _____ while you're in the locker room, but try to keep
    ADJECTIVE
it brief. It's _____ awkward to have a conversation with
                ADVERB
someone while their _____ are on display for everyone
                     PART OF THE BODY (PLURAL)
to see. Likewise, try not to stare if someone is hanging out in their
birthday _____. It doesn't matter if their _____
         ARTICLE OF CLOTHING   PART OF THE BODY
is huge, they have a totally _____ mole, or you would die
                              ADJECTIVE
for those _____-hard abs: Force yourself to look away after
           NOUN
_____ seconds. If you must _____ on your cell
 NUMBER   VERB
phone, make it quick. And above all, remember that you are in a
public place, not in your own _____-room at home!
                               NOUN

From ADULT MAD LIBS™: No Pain, No Gain Mad Libs • Copyright © 2014 by Price Stern Sloan, an imprint of Penguin Group (USA) LLC, 345 Hudson Street, New York, NY 10014.

Adult MAD LIBS™

The world's greatest _fitness_ game

GET YOUR $!* TO THE GYM

MAD LIBS® is fun to play with friends, but you can also play it by yourself! To begin with, DO NOT look at the story on the page below. Fill in the blanks on this page with the words called for. Then, using the words you have selected, fill in the blank spaces in the story. Now you've created your own hilarious MAD LIBS® game!

PART OF THE BODY _____

ADJECTIVE _____

PLURAL NOUN _____

NUMBER _____

TYPE OF FOOD _____

PERSON IN ROOM _____

NOUN _____

ADJECTIVE _____

PART OF THE BODY _____

VERB ENDING IN "ING" _____

NOUN _____

NUMBER _____

NOUN _____

NUMBER _____

ADJECTIVE _____

ADJECTIVE _____

NUMBER _____

GET YOUR $!* TO THE GYM

In need of some motivation to get your _____ to the
                                      PART OF THE BODY
gym? Check out this _____ list. Chances are, one of these
                         ADJECTIVE
_____ applies to you.
 PLURAL NOUN

- Your high-school reunion is in _____ weeks, and the boy
                                      NUMBER
  who called you "_____ _____" will be there.
                   TYPE OF FOOD   PERSON IN ROOM

- You're marrying the _____ of your life and you want the
                           NOUN
  wedding pics to showcase your _____ face, not your giant
                                   ADJECTIVE
  _____.
  PART OF THE BODY

- _____-suit season is right around the _____.
  VERB ENDING IN "ING"   NOUN

- The _____-pack stomach you had in college has turned
         NUMBER
  into a keg.

- Your Ok-_____ profile claims you are _____
              NOUN   NUMBER
  pounds and of _____ build . . . and you don't want your
                   ADJECTIVE
  _____ date to think you're someone else.
   ADJECTIVE

- You pay _____ dollars a month for that gym
              NUMBER
  membership, dammit!

From ADULT MAD LIBS™: No Pain, No Gain Mad Libs • Copyright © 2014 by Price Stern Sloan, an imprint of Penguin Group (USA) LLC, 345 Hudson Street, New York, NY 10014.

Adult MAD LIBS™

DRESS TO IMPRESS

The world's greatest _fitness_ game

MAD LIBS® is fun to play with friends, but you can also play it by yourself! To begin with, DO NOT look at the story on the page below. Fill in the blanks on this page with the words called for. Then, using the words you have selected, fill in the blank spaces in the story. Now you've created your own hilarious MAD LIBS® game!

PART OF THE BODY _____

ARTICLE OF CLOTHING (PLURAL) _____

ADJECTIVE _____

NOUN _____

NOUN _____

ADJECTIVE _____

PART OF THE BODY _____

TYPE OF FOOD _____

VERB _____

ARTICLE OF CLOTHING _____

PART OF THE BODY (PLURAL) _____

ADJECTIVE _____

PLURAL NOUN _____

ADJECTIVE _____

VERB ENDING IN "ING" _____

NOUN _____

Adult MAD LIBS™
The world's greatest _fitness_ game

DRESS TO IMPRESS

Gone are the days of _____-stained T-shirts and tube
                          PART OF THE BODY

_____ at the gym. If you want to look _____
ARTICLE OF CLOTHING (PLURAL)   ADJECTIVE

while you're climbing the _____-Master or impress that cute
                                  NOUN

_____ on the elliptical, you've gotta gear up. Ladies, show off
    NOUN

what you work so hard for in _____ spandex pants and a/an
                                     ADJECTIVE

_____-revealing top. Bonus points if it's Lulu-_____.
PART OF THE BODY   TYPE OF FOOD

Just make sure that you do the _____-over test in the mirror
                                      VERB

before leaving the locker room—you don't want anyone seeing

that cute lacy _____ you've got on! Guys, flaunt your
                ARTICLE OF CLOTHING

ripped _____ in a sleeveless T-shirt. It's okay to show
       PART OF THE BODY (PLURAL)

some skin, but do us all a favor and leave the _____-shorts
                                                    ADJECTIVE

at home. And under no circumstances should you work out in

jeans or cargo _____. The most _____ element of
                PLURAL NOUN   ADJECTIVE

_____ to impress at the gym is confidence. If you think
VERB ENDING IN "ING"

you're the _____, chances are other people will, too!
              NOUN

Adult MAD LIBS

MEETING SOMEONE AT THE GYM

The world's greatest *fitness* game

MAD LIBS® is fun to play with friends, but you can also play it by yourself! To begin with, DO NOT look at the story on the page below. Fill in the blanks on this page with the words called for. Then, using the words you have selected, fill in the blank spaces in the story. Now you've created your own hilarious MAD LIBS® game!

PART OF THE BODY _____

A PLACE _____

ADJECTIVE _____

PART OF THE BODY _____

NOUN _____

ADJECTIVE _____

NOUN _____

NOUN _____

ADVERB _____

ADJECTIVE _____

TYPE OF FOOD _____

PLURAL NOUN _____

NOUN _____

VERB _____

MEETING SOMEONE AT THE GYM

The world's greatest _fitness_ game

So you love working out and want to meet someone who enjoys _____ curls just as much as you do? You're not going to
_{PART OF THE BODY}

meet them in line at (the) _____, that's for sure! Follow this
_{A PLACE}

_____ advice, and you'll be taking your workout buddy home
_{ADJECTIVE}

with you in no time:

- Make eye contact, not _____ contact. Nobody wants to
  _{PART OF THE BODY}

  feel like a piece of _____ . . . even if they *are* wearing next
  _{NOUN}

  to nothing.

- Introduce yourself in a/an _____ way by offering to spot
  _{ADJECTIVE}

  your potential _____ on the bench press.
  _{NOUN}

- Don't ask them out on a/an _____ immediately. Chat
  _{NOUN}

  them up _____ over a couple of weeks, and when the
  _{ADVERB}

  time is _____, ask if they want to grab a/an
  _{ADJECTIVE}

  _____ after spin class.
  _{TYPE OF FOOD}

- Don't get caught talking to other _____ in the weight
  _{PLURAL NOUN}

  room. You don't want your future soul _____ to think
  _{NOUN}

  you're using the gym as your own personal _____.com.
  _{VERB}

_{From ADULT MAD LIBS™: No Pain, No Gain Mad Libs • Copyright © 2014 by Price Stern Sloan, an imprint of Penguin Group (USA) LLC, 345 Hudson Street, New York, NY 10014.}

Adult MAD LIBS™

SO YOU THINK YOU CAN YOGA

The world's greatest _fitness_ game

MAD LIBS® is fun to play with friends, but you can also play it by yourself! To begin with, DO NOT look at the story on the page below. Fill in the blanks on this page with the words called for. Then, using the words you have selected, fill in the blank spaces in the story. Now you've created your own hilarious MAD LIBS® game!

ADVERB _____

ADJECTIVE _____

NOUN _____

ANIMAL _____

PART OF THE BODY _____

PART OF THE BODY _____

PLURAL NOUN _____

NOUN _____

VERB _____

ANIMAL _____

PART OF THE BODY _____

ANIMAL _____

TYPE OF FOOD _____

ADJECTIVE _____

SO YOU THINK YOU CAN YOGA

For first timers, yoga may seem like a/an _____ intimidating
_{ADVERB}
way to exercise, but it's actually quite _____ once you get the
_{ADJECTIVE}
hang of it. Before you walk into your first _____ class, here
_{NOUN}
are some basic poses you need to know.

Downward-Facing _____: Stick your _____ up in
_{ANIMAL} _{PART OF THE BODY}
the air, forming an inverted V-shape with your body. Make sure to
check out the nice _____ of the guy in front of you while
_{PART OF THE BODY}
you're at it!

Child's Pose: The perfect pose for relieving the _____ of
_{PLURAL NOUN}
your workday. Lie on the floor with your knees tucked under your
chest and your head resting on the _____ and _____
_{NOUN} _{VERB}
deeply.

Cat-_____: Get on your hands and knees and alternate
_{ANIMAL}
between arching and rounding your _____, just like a/an
_{PART OF THE BODY}
_____ would!
_{ANIMAL}
Now . . . strap on some Lulu-_____—you're on your way to
_{TYPE OF FOOD}
becoming a/an _____ yogi!
_{ADJECTIVE}

From ADULT MAD LIBS™: No Pain, No Gain Mad Libs • Copyright © 2014 by Price Stern Sloan, an imprint of Penguin Group (USA) LLC, 345 Hudson Street, New York, NY 10014.

Adult MAD LIBS™
26.2 TIPS

The world's greatest _fitness_ game

MAD LIBS® is fun to play with friends, but you can also play it by yourself! To begin with, DO NOT look at the story on the page below. Fill in the blanks on this page with the words called for. Then, using the words you have selected, fill in the blank spaces in the story. Now you've created your own hilarious MAD LIBS® game!

NOUN _____

VERB ENDING IN "ING" _____

NOUN _____

NUMBER _____

ADJECTIVE _____

VERB ENDING IN "ING" _____

NUMBER _____

ADVERB _____

TYPE OF FOOD _____

ADJECTIVE _____

ADJECTIVE _____

PLURAL NOUN _____

PART OF THE BODY (PLURAL) _____

ADVERB _____

NUMBER _____

ADJECTIVE _____

PERSON IN ROOM (FEMALE) _____

26.2 TIPS

The world's greatest _fitness_ game

So running a marathon is on your _____ list. You bought
                                    NOUN
a pair of brand-new _____ sneakers, conned your best
                    VERB ENDING IN "ING"
_____ into doing it with you, and paid your _____
    NOUN   NUMBER
dollars to get in. Now what? Here are some tips to get you through
the most _____ sixteen weeks of your life.
          ADJECTIVE

- Find a/an _____ plan that works for you. Don't pick one
            VERB ENDING IN "ING"
  that demands you run _____ miles backward on day one.
                            NUMBER

- Learn how to eat _____. Fuel up before long runs with
                      ADVERB
  a/an _____ smeared with peanut butter and a banana.
       TYPE OF FOOD
  Pasta is your _____ friend—just not *right* before a run!
                  ADJECTIVE

- Invest in _____-quality running gear, preferably
              ADJECTIVE
  something that wicks your _____ away. Chafed
                                PLURAL NOUN
  _____ are no fun!
  PART OF THE BODY (PLURAL)

- Increase your mileage _____. That means no more than
                           ADVERB
  _____ percent each week!
     NUMBER

- Take a/an _____ break if you feel burned-out. You're
              ADJECTIVE
  not going to win, so don't train like you're _____ Goucher!
                                               PERSON IN ROOM (FEMALE)

From ADULT MAD LIBS™: No Pain, No Gain Mad Libs • Copyright © 2014 by Price Stern Sloan, an imprint of Penguin Group (USA) LLC, 345 Hudson Street, New York, NY 10014.

Adult MAD LIBS

EPIC WORKOUT PLAYLIST

The world's greatest *fitness* game

MAD LIBS® is fun to play with friends, but you can also play it by yourself! To begin with, DO NOT look at the story on the page below. Fill in the blanks on this page with the words called for. Then, using the words you have selected, fill in the blank spaces in the story. Now you've created your own hilarious MAD LIBS® game!

ADJECTIVE _____

VERB ENDING IN "ING" _____

CITY _____

ANIMAL _____

NOUN _____

ARTICLE OF CLOTHING _____

TYPE OF FOOD _____

NUMBER _____

NOUN _____

ADJECTIVE _____

COLOR _____

ADJECTIVE _____

NOUN _____

A PLACE _____

ADJECTIVE _____

PLURAL NOUN _____

EPIC WORKOUT PLAYLIST

The world's greatest *fitness* game

Music can be instant motivation to exercise, if you choose _____ songs. Here's a list of classic workout songs that make
<small>ADJECTIVE</small>

_____ on the treadmill feel like you're crossing the finish line
<small>VERB ENDING IN "ING"</small>

at the _____ Marathon:
<small>CITY</small>

"Eye of the _____": It might be cheesy, but this
<small>ANIMAL</small>

_____ will make you want to break out your best sweat-
<small>NOUN</small>

_____ and go for a jog.
<small>ARTICLE OF CLOTHING</small>

"The Distance": _____'s only hit is perfect for those times
<small>TYPE OF FOOD</small>

when you need to run _____ miles for marathon training.
<small>NUMBER</small>

"Another One Bites the Dust": For maximum workout efficiency,

listen to this _____ on repeat at a/an _____ volume.
<small>NOUN</small>   <small>ADJECTIVE</small>

"Lose Yourself": Eminem may be _____, but he knows how
<small>COLOR</small>

to write a/an _____ rap song. You'll "lose yourself" in your
<small>ADJECTIVE</small>

workout when listening to this _____.
<small>NOUN</small>

"Welcome to (the) _____": Because it's _____
<small>A PLACE</small>   <small>ADJECTIVE</small>

to listen to the same music your dad listened to when lifting

_____.
<small>PLURAL NOUN</small>

<small>From ADULT MAD LIBS™: No Pain, No Gain Mad Libs • Copyright © 2014 by Price Stern Sloan, an imprint of Penguin Group (USA) LLC, 345 Hudson Street, New York, NY 10014.</small>

Adult MAD LIBS

IS PERSONAL TRAINING RIGHT FOR YOU?

The world's greatest _fitness_ game

MAD LIBS® is fun to play with friends, but you can also play it by yourself! To begin with, DO NOT look at the story on the page below. Fill in the blanks on this page with the words called for. Then, using the words you have selected, fill in the blank spaces in the story. Now you've created your own hilarious MAD LIBS® game!

PLURAL NOUN _____

NOUN _____

A PLACE _____

PLURAL NOUN _____

ADJECTIVE _____

NOUN _____

ADVERB _____

ARTICLE OF CLOTHING _____

A PLACE _____

NOUN _____

NUMBER _____

ADVERB _____

PLURAL NOUN _____

ADJECTIVE _____

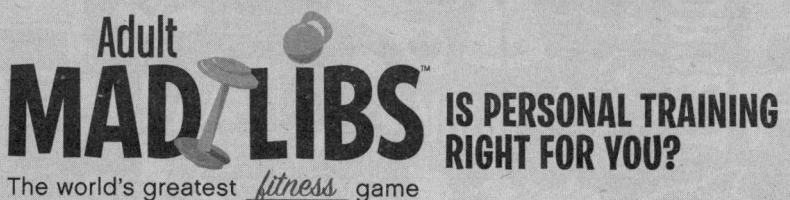

IS PERSONAL TRAINING RIGHT FOR YOU?

Is a personal trainer *really* worth the _____ you have to
                                      PLURAL NOUN
spend? Couldn't you just look up some exercises on your
i-_____ and do them yourself at (the) _____? If
   NOUN   A PLACE
any of the following apply to you, better start saving your
_____—you're in _____ need of a personal trainer.
PLURAL NOUN   ADJECTIVE

- You watch *The Biggest* _____ for inspiration to work
                              NOUN
  out and wind up eating bowl after bowl of ice cream while
  laughing _____ at the contestants' misery.
            ADVERB

- When you gain weight and your _____ no longer
                                   ARTICLE OF CLOTHING
  fits, you don't stress. You simply run to (the) _____
                                                     A PLACE
  and buy a bigger one.

- You make a monthly appearance at the gym for _____
                                                    NOUN
  class, but only because you pay _____ dollars a month for
                                     NUMBER
  your membership.

- You _____ take the elevator to your second-floor
       ADVERB
  apartment . . . and don't even care that your _____ give
                                                  PLURAL NOUN
  you _____ looks.
       ADJECTIVE

From ADULT MAD LIBS™: No Pain, No Gain Mad Libs • Copyright © 2014 by Price Stern Sloan, an imprint of Penguin Group (USA) LLC, 345 Hudson Street, New York, NY 10014.

Adult MAD LIBS I SPY

The world's greatest _fitness_ game

MAD LIBS® is fun to play with friends, but you can also play it by yourself! To begin with, DO NOT look at the story on the page below. Fill in the blanks on this page with the words called for. Then, using the words you have selected, fill in the blank spaces in the story. Now you've created your own hilarious MAD LIBS® game!

ADJECTIVE _____

PART OF THE BODY _____

PLURAL NOUN _____

ADJECTIVE _____

PLURAL NOUN _____

PLURAL NOUN _____

ADJECTIVE _____

ADJECTIVE _____

TYPE OF FOOD _____

CELEBRITY _____

NOUN _____

PLURAL NOUN _____

PART OF THE BODY _____

ADJECTIVE _____

CITY _____

NOUN _____

I SPY

The gym isn't just for working out. It's also a/an _____ (ADJECTIVE) place to see and be seen. If you keep a sharp _____ (PART OF THE BODY) out, you'll be able to spot one or more of these types of _____ (PLURAL NOUN) who hang out at every gym. **The Meathead** is the big _____ (ADJECTIVE) guy who grunts while he lifts _____ (PLURAL NOUN). He's also the guy who checks out his own _____ (PLURAL NOUN) in the mirror. **The Model** is the _____ (ADJECTIVE), beautiful girl who works out in nothing but a sports bra and _____ (ADJECTIVE) shorts. In other words, the person who makes you want to pack it all in and just go home to eat a giant tub of _____ (TYPE OF FOOD). **Inappropriate Outfit Guy** wears full-on spandex to spin class. You're not _____ (CELEBRITY), buddy. And nobody wants to see your _____ (NOUN). Well . . . except maybe for **the Cougar**, who comes to the gym on the hunt for fresh _____ (PLURAL NOUN). She usually wears a coordinating outfit, a full _____ (PART OF THE BODY) of makeup, and a/an _____ (ADJECTIVE) gleam in her eye. Beware! **Newspaper Guy** pedals on the stationary bike while reading the _____ (CITY) *Times*. Listen up, guy: It's not exercise if you're not breaking a/an _____ (NOUN)!

Adult MAD LIBS

EXERCISE ANYWHERE

The world's greatest _fitness_ game

MAD LIBS® is fun to play with friends, but you can also play it by yourself! To begin with, DO NOT look at the story on the page below. Fill in the blanks on this page with the words called for. Then, using the words you have selected, fill in the blank spaces in the story.

Now you've created your own hilarious MAD LIBS® game!

ADJECTIVE _____

PLURAL NOUN _____

ADJECTIVE _____

ADJECTIVE _____

ADJECTIVE _____

PART OF THE BODY _____

VERB _____

ADJECTIVE _____

A PLACE _____

VERB _____

NOUN _____

NOUN _____

NUMBER _____

PART OF THE BODY (PLURAL) _____

EXERCISE ANYWHERE

So you're too _____ (ADJECTIVE) to get yourself a gym membership, but you still want to lose those few extra _____ (PLURAL NOUN)? You don't need a gym with fancy equipment to get a/an _____ (ADJECTIVE) workout in—you've got the _____ (ADJECTIVE) outdoors. The most _____ (ADJECTIVE) thing you can do outside is jogging. It's easy: Just put one _____ (PART OF THE BODY) in front of the other and _____ (VERB) until you can't feel your legs anymore. If you really want to be _____ (ADJECTIVE), try to vary your speed: Find a stoplight ahead of you and sprint as fast as you can until you reach it. Or why don't you head to your local _____ (A PLACE) to try some exercises using your own body weight, like _____ (VERB)-ups or crunches. Some parks even have equipment intended for specific exercises, like pull-ups. Just don't try it on the kids' jungle gym, or you'll have the _____ (NOUN) chasing after you! If you're so lazy or antisocial that you don't feel like leaving your _____ (NOUN), clear a space in front of your TV and pop in an exercise DVD like the _____ (NUMBER)-Day Shred. With enough persistence, people will wonder where you got your ripped _____ (PART OF THE BODY (PLURAL))!

Adult MAD LIBS™
THE DANGERS OF SPIN CLASS

The world's greatest *fitness* game

MAD LIBS® is fun to play with friends, but you can also play it by yourself! To begin with, DO NOT look at the story on the page below. Fill in the blanks on this page with the words called for. Then, using the words you have selected, fill in the blank spaces in the story. Now you've created your own hilarious MAD LIBS® game!

ADJECTIVE _____

ADJECTIVE _____

PLURAL NOUN _____

PART OF THE BODY _____

NUMBER _____

PART OF THE BODY _____

ANIMAL (PLURAL) _____

ADJECTIVE _____

NUMBER _____

OCCUPATION _____

ADJECTIVE _____

ADJECTIVE _____

NOUN _____

PART OF THE BODY (PLURAL) _____

VERB ENDING IN "ING" _____

NOUN _____

THE DANGERS OF SPIN CLASS

Spinning is one of the most _____ ways to exercise. You get
                                 ADJECTIVE
to work out in the dark and listen to _____ music. But it isn't
                                       ADJECTIVE
all fun and _____. Beware of these dangers:
            PLURAL NOUN

- _____ **soreness.** After spending _____ minutes
  PART OF THE BODY   NUMBER
  on a hard plastic bike seat, your _____ is bound to feel
                                    PART OF THE BODY
  like it's been attacked by a gang of wild _____.
                                             ANIMAL (PLURAL)

- **Chafing.** Don't wear shorts to spin class unless you want to walk
  around with a/an _____ raw feeling between your legs for
                   ADJECTIVE
  the next _____ days.
           NUMBER

- **Boredom.** If your _____ totally sucks, it's going to feel
                       OCCUPATION
  like the most _____ forty-five minutes of your life. Bonus
                ADJECTIVE
  points if he plays music that was only _____ in the
                                          ADJECTIVE
  eighties.

- **Confusion.** There's a good chance that the next time
  you're riding your _____ outside you may close your
                     NOUN
  _____ and start _____ your cadence. Just
  PART OF THE BODY (PLURAL) VERB ENDING IN "ING"
  make sure you're wearing a/an _____.
                                 NOUN

From ADULT MAD LIBS™: No Pain, No Gain Mad Libs • Copyright © 2014 by Price Stern Sloan, an imprint of Penguin Group (USA) LLC, 345 Hudson Street, New York, NY 10014.

Adult MAD LIBS

BAD ETIQUETTE IN THE WEIGHT ROOM

The world's greatest *fitness* game

MAD LIBS® is fun to play with friends, but you can also play it by yourself! To begin with, DO NOT look at the story on the page below. Fill in the blanks on this page with the words called for. Then, using the words you have selected, fill in the blank spaces in the story. Now you've created your own hilarious MAD LIBS® game!

SILLY WORD _____

NOUN _____

PLURAL NOUN _____

ANIMAL _____

VERB ENDING IN "ING" _____

NOUN _____

ADJECTIVE _____

NUMBER _____

VERB ENDING IN "ING" _____

ADVERB _____

PLURAL NOUN _____

ADJECTIVE _____

NOUN _____

PLURAL NOUN _____

VERB _____

NOUN _____

VERB _____

BAD ETIQUETTE IN THE WEIGHT ROOM

Listen up, _____ (SILLY WORD)—you're not the only one in the weight room. To avoid looking like a total _____ (NOUN)-bag while you work on your _____ (PLURAL NOUN), make sure to do the following:

- Clean up after yourself, you sweaty _____ (ANIMAL). Wipe down your equipment before _____ (VERB ENDING IN "ING") on to the next _____ (NOUN).

- Keep any _____ (ADJECTIVE) noises to yourself. Sure, you've got _____ (NUMBER) pounds on your bar. But the whole gym doesn't need to know what you sound like when you're _____ (VERB ENDING IN "ING") your girlfriend.

- Don't _____ (ADVERB) interrupt everybody you see to ask how many _____ (PLURAL NOUN) they have left. It's _____ (ADJECTIVE) if you need to work in a set here and there, but don't be that _____ (NOUN) who kicks everybody off their _____ (PLURAL NOUN).

- Similarly, be willing to _____ (VERB) your machine if somebody asks. Unless they're a/an _____ (NOUN)-bag, in which case—tell them to _____ (VERB) off.

Adult MAD LIBS

1-800-GET-BIGG!

The world's greatest _fitness_ game

MAD LIBS® is fun to play with friends, but you can also play it by yourself! To begin with, DO NOT look at the story on the page below. Fill in the blanks on this page with the words called for. Then, using the words you have selected, fill in the blank spaces in the story.

Now you've created your own hilarious MAD LIBS® game!

NOUN _____

PART OF THE BODY (PLURAL) _____

NOUN _____

ADJECTIVE _____

CELEBRITY _____

ADJECTIVE _____

NUMBER _____

ADJECTIVE _____

ADJECTIVE _____

TYPE OF LIQUID _____

VERB _____

ADJECTIVE _____

PART OF THE BODY _____

NOUN _____

PART OF THE BODY _____

ADJECTIVE _____

TYPE OF LIQUID _____

ADJECTIVE _____

Adult MAD LIBS

1-800-GET-BIGG!

The world's greatest *fitness* game

Want to transform your body without doing a/an _____
NOUN
of work? Do you dream about having _____ as big as
PART OF THE BODY (PLURAL)
the _____'s and legs as _____ as _____'s?
NOUN   ADJECTIVE   CELEBRITY
It's as _____ as one, two, _____! Simply call our
ADJECTIVE   NUMBER
toll-free number for a free sample of the most _____ new
ADJECTIVE
product to hit the market in years. Big Gunzz is a/an _____
ADJECTIVE
powder that, when mixed with _____ and consumed before,
TYPE OF LIQUID
during, and after your workout, will _____ away your fat
VERB
and build _____ muscle—guaranteed! Side effects include:
ADJECTIVE
acne on your _____, decrease in _____ drive, and a
PART OF THE BODY   NOUN
shrinking _____. Do not take when operating _____
PART OF THE BODY   ADJECTIVE
machinery or under the influence of _____. Why wait—
TYPE OF LIQUID
GET _____ NOW!!!
ADJECTIVE

Adult MAD LIBS

CROSSFIT KOOL-AID

The world's greatest *fitness* game

MAD LIBS® is fun to play with friends, but you can also play it by yourself! To begin with, DO NOT look at the story on the page below. Fill in the blanks on this page with the words called for. Then, using the words you have selected, fill in the blank spaces in the story. Now you've created your own hilarious MAD LIBS® game!

ADJECTIVE _____

TYPE OF FOOD _____

SAME TYPE OF FOOD _____

ADVERB _____

PLURAL NOUN _____

ADJECTIVE _____

VERB ENDING IN "ING" _____

NOUN _____

VERB (PAST TENSE) _____

PART OF THE BODY _____

NOUN _____

OCCUPATION _____

ADJECTIVE _____

PART OF THE BODY _____

PLURAL NOUN _____

VERB _____

VERB _____

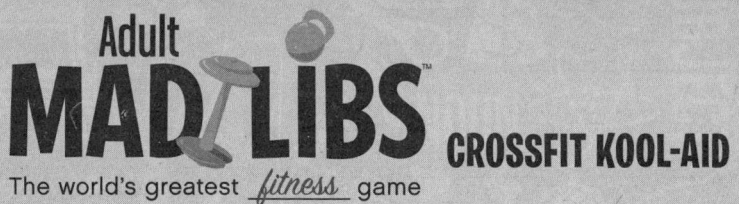

CROSSFIT KOOL-AID

The world's greatest _fitness_ game

CrossFit is the most _____ thing since sliced _____
                          ADJECTIVE   TYPE OF FOOD

(as long as the _____ is Paleo). Worried that you're
                  SAME TYPE OF FOOD

_____ addicted and your friends and _____ might
   ADVERB   PLURAL NOUN

stage an intervention? Here are some _____ signs you've been
                                         ADJECTIVE

_____ the CrossFit Kool-Aid . . .
VERB ENDING IN "ING"

- The first thing you do when you wake up is look on the

  _____ to see if the WOD has been _____.
     NOUN   VERB (PAST TENSE)

- You've compared _____ bruises and _____ burns
                   PART OF THE BODY   NOUN

  with a friend.

- You use the word _Rx_ more often than a/an _____.
                                                 OCCUPATION

- You got a/an _____ tattoo of a kettlebell on your
                  ADJECTIVE

  _____ and love to show it off.
  PART OF THE BODY

- You've divided your _____ into CrossFitters and
                        PLURAL NOUN

  non-CrossFitters . . . and you would _never_ _____ a
                                                    VERB

  non-CrossFitter. Never.

- If you meet someone named Fran, you _____ in the other
                                          VERB

  direction.

From ADULT MAD LIBS™: No Pain, No Gain Mad Libs • Copyright © 2014 by Price Stern Sloan, an imprint of Penguin Group (USA) LLC, 345 Hudson Street, New York, NY 10014.

Adult MAD LIBS
The world's greatest *fitness* game

GYM BAG ESSENTIALS

MAD LIBS® is fun to play with friends, but you can also play it by yourself! To begin with, DO NOT look at the story on the page below. Fill in the blanks on this page with the words called for. Then, using the words you have selected, fill in the blank spaces in the story. Now you've created your own hilarious MAD LIBS® game!

ADJECTIVE _____

ANIMAL _____

ADJECTIVE _____

A PLACE _____

NOUN _____

ADJECTIVE _____

PLURAL NOUN _____

NOUN _____

ADJECTIVE _____

PLURAL NOUN _____

ADJECTIVE _____

NOUN _____

PART OF THE BODY _____

VERB _____

ADJECTIVE _____

PART OF THE BODY _____

ADJECTIVE _____

VERB _____

Adult MAD LIBS

The world's greatest *fitness* game

GYM BAG ESSENTIALS

Every _____ gym-_____ should carry a gym bag
         ADJECTIVE   ANIMAL

filled with essentials. This is especially _____ if you like to
                                                ADJECTIVE

work out in the morning before you head to (the) _____
                                                        A PLACE

or at lunch during your _____ break. You'll be prepared for
                              NOUN

any _____ situation if you stock your bag with the following
       ADJECTIVE

_____:
  PLURAL NOUN

- **Toiletries:** Pack your own shampoo, conditioner, and

  _____ wash, or you'll be stuck using the _____
        NOUN   ADJECTIVE

  soap in the gym showers. Ew—who wants to smell like

  _____ all day?
    PLURAL NOUN

- **A towel:** If you're _____ enough to go to a gym that
                              ADJECTIVE

  actually *provides* towels, they will probably be _____-
                                                          NOUN

  size. If you want to cover more than your _____, bring
                                                 PART OF THE BODY

  your own.

- _____-flops: A/An _____ case of athlete's
       VERB   ADJECTIVE

  _____ is never _____. Pack a pair of cheap
   PART OF THE BODY   ADJECTIVE

  sandals or _____ to regret it.
                   VERB

Adult
MAD LIBS
WORKOUT 101

The world's greatest _fitness_ game

MAD LIBS® is fun to play with friends, but you can also play it by yourself! To begin with, DO NOT look at the story on the page below. Fill in the blanks on this page with the words called for. Then, using the words you have selected, fill in the blank spaces in the story. Now you've created your own hilarious MAD LIBS® game!

NUMBER _____

ADJECTIVE _____

NOUN _____

ADJECTIVE _____

NOUN _____

ADJECTIVE _____

ARTICLE OF CLOTHING _____

PART OF THE BODY (PLURAL) _____

VERB _____

VERB _____

ADJECTIVE _____

NOUN _____

ADJECTIVE _____

PLURAL NOUN _____

WORKOUT 101

The world's greatest _fitness_ game

You may think that the _____ dollars you pay every month
NUMBER

entitles you to act like a/an _____ _____ at the gym,
ADJECTIVE   NOUN

but think again. Here's a list of things to do and NOT to do at the

gym in order to make your time there as _____ as possible:
ADJECTIVE

Do wipe down your _____ after every use.
NOUN

Don't wipe it down with your _____, stinky
ADJECTIVE

_____—gross!
ARTICLE OF CLOTHING

Do say hello to all the familiar _____ you see.
PART OF THE BODY (PLURAL)

Don't completely ignore everyone and _____ as loudly as
VERB

you can on your cell phone while walking on the treadmill.

Do allow others to work in a set, if they _____ politely.
VERB

Don't pretend not to hear them and then get _____ if
ADJECTIVE

someone takes too long on a/an _____ you want to use.
NOUN

Do put on _____ clothes and deodorant before hitting
ADJECTIVE

the gym.

Don't douse your entire body with eau de _____ before
PLURAL NOUN

a workout!

From ADULT MAD LIBS™: No Pain, No Gain Mad Libs • Copyright © 2014 by Price Stern Sloan, an imprint of Penguin Group (USA) LLC, 345 Hudson Street, New York, NY 10014.

Adult MAD LIBS™

GET FIT WITH MAD LIBS

The world's greatest *fitness* game

MAD LIBS® is fun to play with friends, but you can also play it by yourself! To begin with, DO NOT look at the story on the page below. Fill in the blanks on this page with the words called for. Then, using the words you have selected, fill in the blank spaces in the story. Now you've created your own hilarious MAD LIBS® game!

NOUN _____

PLURAL NOUN _____

PART OF THE BODY _____

ADJECTIVE _____

NUMBER _____

VERB ENDING IN "ING" _____

ADJECTIVE _____

ADJECTIVE _____

VERB _____

NUMBER _____

ADJECTIVE _____

PART OF THE BODY _____

PART OF THE BODY (PLURAL) _____

PART OF THE BODY _____

VERB _____

NUMBER _____

NOUN _____

GET FIT WITH MAD LIBS

The world's greatest _fitness_ game

Do you dream of having _____-hard abs, ripped
                              NOUN

_____, and a tiny little _____? Follow this quick and
PLURAL NOUN   PART OF THE BODY

easy workout, and you're sure to see _____ results in no time!
                                          ADJECTIVE

- First, warm up for _____ minutes by _____
                          NUMBER   VERB ENDING IN "ING"

  lightly on the treadmill.

- After your body is nice and _____, grab a pair of
                                   ADJECTIVE

  dumbbells for your first exercise, a/an _____-bell squat.
                                              ADJECTIVE

  _____ down as low as you can twenty times.
  VERB

- Next, drop down to the floor for _____ push-ups.
                                        NUMBER

- After that, try a Romanian _____-lift using your
                                  ADJECTIVE

  dumbbells. Lower your hands all the way to the floor while

  bending at your _____. Squeeze your _____
                     PART OF THE BODY   PART OF THE BODY (PLURAL)

  when you come back up. Try fifteen reps.

- Next, perform a standing dumbbell _____ press. Hold
                                         PART OF THE BODY

  a weight in each hand and _____ up.
                                 VERB

- Repeat the entire workout _____ more times, and finish
                                 NUMBER

  with twenty minutes of cardio on the stationary _____.
                                                       NOUN

Adult MAD LIBS

YOU ARE WHAT YOU EAT

The world's greatest _fitness_ game

MAD LIBS® is fun to play with friends, but you can also play it by yourself! To begin with, DO NOT look at the story on the page below. Fill in the blanks on this page with the words called for. Then, using the words you have selected, fill in the blank spaces in the story. Now you've created your own hilarious MAD LIBS® game!

ADJECTIVE _____

A PLACE _____

ADJECTIVE _____

CELEBRITY _____

ADJECTIVE _____

NOUN _____

TYPE OF LIQUID _____

ADJECTIVE _____

TYPE OF FOOD _____

PLURAL NOUN _____

COLOR _____

ADJECTIVE _____

PERSON IN ROOM (MALE) _____

NOUN _____

ADJECTIVE _____

ADJECTIVE _____

VERB _____

ADJECTIVE _____

Adult MAD LIBS

The world's greatest _fitness_ game

YOU ARE WHAT YOU EAT

You know the _____ saying: Abs are made in the kitchen,
                    ADJECTIVE

not in (the) _____! If you're wondering why you're not
              A PLACE

as _____ as _____ despite the hours you spend
   ADJECTIVE   CELEBRITY

at the gym, it's probably because of your _____ diet. A
                                           ADJECTIVE

really fit _____ drinks a lot of _____. You need to
            NOUN   TYPE OF LIQUID

replenish all the fluids that you lose while working out, and the

best way to do it is _____ old-fashioned H₂0! And no, beer
                      ADJECTIVE

doesn't count as a liquid. Chances are you're eating way too many

carbohydrates. Instead of cereal for breakfast, a/an _____
                                                      TYPE OF FOOD

sandwich for lunch, and spaghetti and _____ for dinner,
                                        PLURAL NOUN

and eat more protein and _____ vegetables! You don't have
                           COLOR

to eat a/an _____ steak for every meal like _____
             ADJECTIVE   PERSON IN ROOM (MALE)

Flintstone, either. Eggs, Greek yogurt, and _____ butter are
                                              NOUN

all _____ sources of protein. Finally, make sure to avoid fatty,
     ADJECTIVE

_____ foods, and _____ in moderation. The next
 ADJECTIVE   VERB

time someone asks you if you want to _____-size it, just say
                                       ADJECTIVE

no!

From ADULT MAD LIBS™: No Pain, No Gain Mad Libs • Copyright © 2014 by Price Stern Sloan, an imprint of Penguin Group (USA) LLC, 345 Hudson Street, New York, NY 10014.

Adult MAD LIBS

AS SEEN ON TV

The world's greatest *fitness* game

MAD LIBS® is fun to play with friends, but you can also play it by yourself! To begin with, DO NOT look at the story on the page below. Fill in the blanks on this page with the words called for. Then, using the words you have selected, fill in the blank spaces in the story. Now you've created your own hilarious MAD LIBS® game!

ADJECTIVE _____

PLURAL NOUN _____

ADJECTIVE _____

PART OF THE BODY (PLURAL) _____

ADJECTIVE _____

VERB _____

VERB ENDING IN "ING" _____

NOUN _____

ADJECTIVE _____

NOUN _____

PART OF THE BODY _____

PART OF THE BODY _____

ADJECTIVE _____

AS SEEN ON TV

Does it seem too _____ to be true? Then it probably is!
ADJECTIVE

You may think these _____ will help you get fit in no
PLURAL NOUN

time, but the truth is, they're as _____ as Kim Kardashian's
ADJECTIVE

_____.
PART OF THE BODY (PLURAL)

Shake Weight: Claims to build _____ muscles, but let's
ADJECTIVE

be real—the only thing this helps improve is the amount of time

it takes you to _____ while _____ off.
VERB   VERB ENDING IN "ING"

Bender Ball: Sure, this could help make crunches more

challenging. But why spend $19.99 when you can steal your kid's

toy _____ and do the same thing?
NOUN

Belly Burner: If you want a/an _____ stomach, all you
ADJECTIVE

have to do is strap on this _____ and let it work its magic.
NOUN

Right? WRONG! The only thing this belt might do is give your

_____ third-degree burns.
PART OF THE BODY

Sauna Pants: It's like a sauna . . . but for your _____.
PART OF THE BODY

Because that's just what you want: to feel all hot and

_____ down there!
ADJECTIVE

From ADULT MAD LIBS™: No Pain, No Gain Mad Libs • Copyright © 2014 by Price Stern Sloan, an imprint of Penguin Group (USA) Inc., 345 Hudson Street, New York, NY 10014.

Adult MAD LIBS™

FITTING IT IN

The world's greatest _fitness_ game

MAD LIBS® is fun to play with friends, but you can also play it by yourself! To begin with, DO NOT look at the story on the page below. Fill in the blanks on this page with the words called for. Then, using the words you have selected, fill in the blank spaces in the story. Now you've created your own hilarious MAD LIBS® game!

ADJECTIVE _____

ADJECTIVE _____

ANIMAL _____

ADJECTIVE _____

NOUN _____

PART OF THE BODY _____

VERB _____

PART OF THE BODY _____

NOUN _____

ARTICLE OF CLOTHING _____

NOUN _____

SAME NOUN _____

NOUN _____

NOUN _____

NUMBER _____

ADJECTIVE _____

NOUN _____

FITTING IT IN

One of the most _____ excuses people make for skipping the
                    ADJECTIVE
gym is not having enough _____ time during the day. Talk
                              ADJECTIVE
about a load of _____-you-know-what! If you want to lose
                    ANIMAL
weight and stop feeling like such a fat, _____ _____,
                                              ADJECTIVE   NOUN
just shut your _____ and do it! You might find it easiest to
                PART OF THE BODY
_____ first thing in the morning. Do whatever it takes to get
      VERB
your _____ out of bed when your alarm goes off, like putting
       PART OF THE BODY
your _____ across the room so you're forced to get up, or
          NOUN
wearing your gym _____ to bed. Or try making a date with
                  ARTICLE OF CLOTHING
a friend. You'll look like a total _____ if you stand her up, and
                                        NOUN
no one wants to look like a total _____! If your job allows it,
                                     SAME NOUN
try working out during your _____ hour. It beats sitting at
                                 NOUN
your desk watching _____-flix. When all else fails, head to
                         NOUN
the gym at the end of the day and promise yourself that if you spend
_____ minutes on the elliptical, you'll meet your friends
   NUMBER
afterward for _____ hour. But for only one _____—
                 ADJECTIVE   NOUN
you are trying to lose weight, after all!

From ADULT MAD LIBS™: No Pain, No Gain Mad Libs • Copyright © 2014 by Price Stern Sloan, an imprint of Penguin Group (USA) LLC, 345 Hudson Street, New York, NY 10014.

Adult MAD LIBS™
WORK IT, GIRL!

The world's greatest _fitness_ game

MAD LIBS® is fun to play with friends, but you can also play it by yourself! To begin with, DO NOT look at the story on the page below. Fill in the blanks on this page with the words called for. Then, using the words you have selected, fill in the blank spaces in the story. Now you've created your own hilarious MAD LIBS® game!

PLURAL NOUN _____

ADJECTIVE _____

ADJECTIVE _____

ADJECTIVE _____

NOUN _____

TYPE OF LIQUID _____

ADJECTIVE _____

PLURAL NOUN _____

CELEBRITY _____

SAME CELEBRITY _____

OCCUPATION _____

VERB ENDING IN "ING" _____

NUMBER _____

ADJECTIVE _____

NOUN _____

Adult MAD LIBS™
WORK IT, GIRL!
The world's greatest *fitness* game

Nowadays there are more boutique fitness classes than there are _____ at the zoo! With all the _____ options
    PLURAL NOUN   ADJECTIVE

available, chances are you'll be able to find one that fits your _____ lifestyle. So which class is right for you?
                                           ADJECTIVE

Pilates: You love to look _____ while exercising and
                                        ADJECTIVE

would rather not break a/an _____ because you're headed
                                            NOUN

to happy hour for a glass of _____ right after class.
                                       TYPE OF LIQUID

Barry's Bootcamp: You're totally _____ and have
                                              ADJECTIVE

plenty of _____ to burn, so you prefer to work out like
             PLURAL NOUN

_____ (or *alongside* _____!).
  CELEBRITY   SAME CELEBRITY

Pure Barre: You were a/an _____ in your younger days
                                     OCCUPATION

and still have dreams of _____ onstage at Lincoln Center.
                            VERB ENDING IN "ING"

Physique _____: You love high-intensity cardio
                 NUMBER

and dance, but you're too _____ to take a Zumba or
                               ADJECTIVE

_____-dancing class!
  NOUN

Enjoy more ADULT MAD LIBS™ from
PSS!
PRICE STERN SLOAN

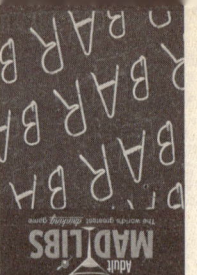

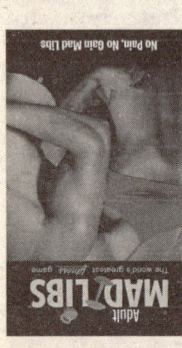

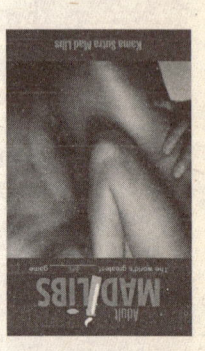